Magic and Mayhem

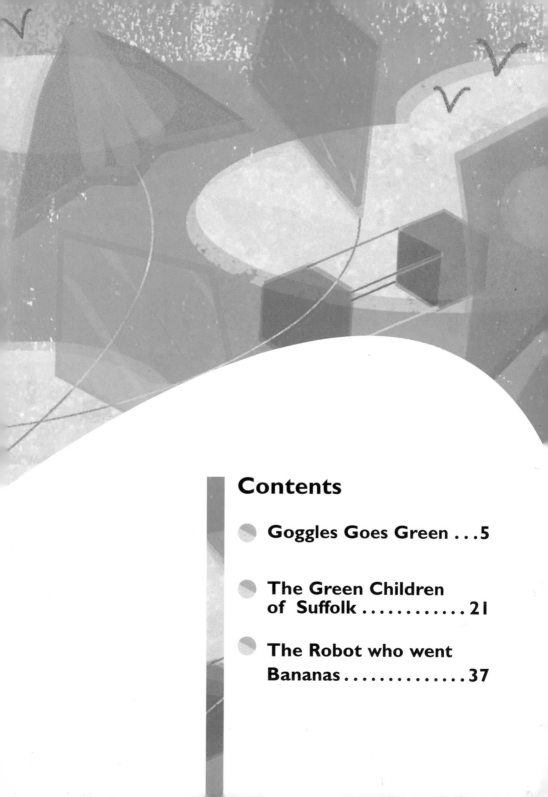

Contents

Goggles Goes Green . . . 5

The Green Children
of Suffolk 21

The Robot who went
Bananas 37

RIGBY

Halley Court, Jordan Hill, Oxford, OX2 8EJ
a division of Harcourt Education Ltd

www.myprimary.co.uk

Help and support for teachers, plus the widest
range of education solutions

Rigby is a registered trademark of Harcourt
Education Ltd

Magic and Mayhem first published 2004

'Goggles Goes Green' © Helen Cresswell
2004

'The Green Children of Suffolk' © Helen
Cresswell 2004

'The Robot who went Bananas' © Ruth
Dowley 2004

Series editor: Shirley Bickler

08 07
10 9 8 7 6 5

Magic and Mayhem
ISBN 0433 035226 /9780433035220
Group reading pack with teaching notes
ISBN 0433 035668 /9780433035664

Illustrated by Kate Sheppard, Rosalind Hudson
and David Whittle

Cover illustration © Sharon Tancredi

Designed by StoreyBooks

Repro by Digital Imaging, Glasgow

Printed and bound in China by CTPS

Goggles Goes Green

written by Helen Cresswell

illustrated by Kate Sheppard

Magic and Mayhem

It was gross. How would you like it? You walk into a room and there's your kid brother, and he's green! Pea green. Green as grass, green as spinach, green as – well, you get the picture.

He's on his computer and looks up. "I thought you were asleep," he says.

It's only six o'clock on a Friday morning, but the sound of Goggles tapping on the keyboard has woken me up.

Goggles looks at me and the whites of his eyes flash. "What's up?" he asks.

Good question. I try to answer, but all that comes out is a croak.

"You all right?" he asks.

I'm all right. He's the one with the problem. I point to the mirror. He looks.

"It's worked!" he says. "I don't believe it!"

Me neither. "What kind of dork wants to spray himself green?" I ask.

"You don't get it," he says. "I really *am* green."

8

He's called Goggles because he's a Harry
Potter freak and chose his specs to look like him.
Wants to be a wizard, he says. Fat chance.

So anyway, it turns out he's been mucking
about on the Internet searching for wizards and
spells.

"It worked! Hey – I am a wizard. I can do
spells!" He punches the air and spins like a mad
green firework.

"You'd better get unspelling," I say. "Mum and Dad'll have a fit."

"Don't care," he says. "They didn't believe I could be a wizard. Now I can prove it."

"Going to school like that, are you?" I ask.

"That lot didn't believe me either," he says. "This'll show them."

"It'll do that all right," I tell him.

Just then there's a horrendous scream. I whip round and there's Mum, though I hardly recognise her. This is horrible. Goggles is green, and now Mum's gone bonkers.

For the first time, Goggles looks worried.

"Mum!" he shouts. "Mum! It's OK. It's cool."

Cool, he says. What does he mean, 'cool'?

Now Dad's here.

"What's up?" he says. Then he sees Goggles.

His eyes bulge and his mouth opens and shuts like a fish.

"He's ill!" shrieks Mum. "We must get a doctor!"

"He's got jaundice," says Dad. "No, that's yellow. Scarlet fever."

"I think you'll find that's red, Dad," I tell him.

"I haven't got *anything*," Goggles says. "I'm a wizard."

Then he tells them.

"Well, you'd better get straight back on the net and undo the spell," Dad tells him.

"No!"

"I will then!" I say.

I go over to the computer.
The screen is just as he left it.

"WIZARD OF WOLF-PITS," I read. "SPELLS." I read down the list. "Hey. It could have been worse. He could have changed himself into a wild boar!"

"No! No!" he yells.

Goggles has darted past Mum and Dad and is heading downstairs. We hear the front door slam. I rush to the window. He's heading through the gate, green legs going like scissors.

That's when all hell breaks loose. The milkman is just walking up the next-door-neighbour's path. He takes one look, drops the bottles and runs. "Help! Help! Invasion from Outer Space!"

A car is coming up the road. Next thing there's a deafening crash. The car has gone right into the back of the milk float.

"Oh no!" Dad groans. He heads for the door with Mum running after him. I can see the car driver on his mobile. He'll be calling the police. Goggles is just standing there, staring at the broken bottles and rivers of milk.

Old Mrs Stokes from number ten has come out now. She takes her specs off, puts them on again, then starts screaming. "EEEEEEEEK!"

I've got to act fast.

I scan the computer screen: TURN GREEN, TURN INTO A WILD BOAR, AN ADDER … There it is! FOR THE UNSPELLING OF SPELLS.

What?????? I've got to do *what*???? I've got to strip naked and spin round three times and chant these crummy words. I can hear voices yelling in the street. Then, in the distance, a police siren.

I whip the t-shirt over my head and do the spinning and chanting. Then I race downstairs and out through the front door.

"Did it work?" I yell.

I stop dead. Now they're all looking at *me*.
For a split second I can't think why. Then ...

I'm back inside in a flash. But not before I've
seen Goggles is back to normal. (If normal's
the word.)

We did tell the police the truth. Goggles took them up to the computer to see for themselves.

Only thing is, the website had gone. Vanished into thin air. Goggles must have tried a thousand times, but he couldn't find it again. So the police didn't believe us. Why would they? Do you?

The Green Children of Suffolk

retold by **Helen Creswell**

illustrated by **Rosalind Hudson**

Long ago in Suffolk, there lived a boy called John. It was his job to look after the sheep near the village of Wolf-pits.

One very hot day, he went to a nearby cave for shade. As he drew near he saw two children sleeping, a boy and a girl. They were as green as the grass they lay on. Faces, arms, legs, feet – all green. John ran as fast as he could back to Wolf-pits.

22

"Quick!" he gasped. "Come quick!"
He told his story, and some men
from the village agreed to go back
to the cave with him. They only
half-believed him.

"Are you sure you weren't
dreaming when you should have been
watching sheep?" asked one.

"If they're green, I'm sky blue!" joked another.

But when they reached the cave, they could hardly believe their eyes.

"They're not human beings!" whispered one.

"Fairies!" gasped another.

The men lifted the sleeping children, and took them back to Wolf-pits. Soon the whole village gathered round, and, as they stared, the children began to wake up.

They seemed terrified. They stared wildly round and shaded their eyes, as if blinded by the sun. Then they began to gabble to each other in a strange language.

"Poor things!" John's mother said. "Perhaps they're hungry."

Some of the women fetched bread and cheese but the green children only cowered back, trembling. They refused everything until, at last, someone fetched a plate of peas. At once the children began to eat, cramming the peas into their mouths.

"Perhaps it's eating green things that has turned them green," John's mother whispered.

But John didn't believe it. This boy and girl were no ordinary humans.

John gave
the green children
names, calling the girl Beth
and the boy Simon. He spent
hours with them, trying to teach
them English.

"Man, woman, plate, sheep," he would
say, pointing to each thing as he named it.
Beth listened, repeating the words. But
Simon turned away and lay curled on
the ground.

Beth began to go out each day with John to watch the sheep, but Simon stayed behind, sad and silent. He was still as green as the day John had first found him, and ate only a handful of peas each day.

One day, John overheard his parents talking.

"That boy's getting thinner and thinner," John's mother said.

"I don't think he's long for this world," his father agreed.

27

John was horrified to think that Simon might die. He went out to where Simon lay curled in his usual place.

"Friend," he said, and took Simon's green hand in his. "I want to help you."

Simon did not seem to understand.

"Tell him," John begged Beth. "Tell him in your own language!" He waited to hear their strange babble.

"He's your friend," Beth told her brother in English. Then she turned to John in amazement.

"I've forgotten our language!" she cried. "I can't seem to speak it! Oh, poor Simon!" She began to cry, hugging her thin green brother in her arms. Now there was no one he could talk to. Poor Simon was more lost and lonely than ever.

"Why won't he eat?" John asked. "Why won't he learn our language? *You* have."

"I think he misses home more than I do," Beth told him. "And he longs for our mother. He was always her favourite."

Suddenly John had an idea. "Let's take him with us to watch the sheep today," he said. "Do you think he can walk that far?"

Together they helped Simon to his feet. They made their way slowly to the field where John had first found the green children. Simon's face brightened a little when he saw the sheep, but then tears began to roll down his green cheeks. He sank to the ground in the field, near the cave, and lay there, gazing at the sheep through his tears.

"He remembers," said Beth softly.

"Remembers what?" John asked. "Tell me. Tell me where you're from. It might be Simon's only hope."

And so, at last, Beth told him their story. Before, she had only shaken her head and stayed silent when asked.

"We come from a place called St Martin's Land," she told him. "There is no sun there. It's always twilight."

"That's why you were blinded by the sun that first day!" John exclaimed.

32

"My brother and I look after the sheep there,"
she said. "Then one day, we heard a ringing of bells."

"Bells?" repeated John.

She nodded. "Lured on by the bells, Simon and
I reached a cave. We followed the sweet sound deep
into the darkness. Then, all at once, we stumbled out
the other side of the cave – and found ourselves in
blinding sunlight."

"And that's where you lay down and slept,"
murmured John.

Beth nodded.

"Then we must get Simon back to St Martin's
Land!" John cried. "We'll take him into the cave
and then he can find his way back home!"

Beth shook her head sadly. "No one who
leaves St Martin's Land can ever return," she said.

John stared at her in horror. He had been so
sure his plan would work.

"And if we stay here, my brother will die."

And so it happened. Simon slowly faded away
and died, pining for the lost land of St Martin's.
But Beth stayed and the greenness faded from
her skin. And she spent the rest of her days in
Wolf-pits.

The Robot who went Bananas

written by **Ruth Dowley**

illustrated by **David Whittle**

Characters

Hoov

Narrator
Also reads the part of the
Information Service Voice

Pete

Jenny

Mum

Dad

Scene

one

Narrator	*The year is 2040. On her way home from work, Mum has picked up Pete and Jenny from school in the electric car. Pete and Jenny run through the house to the activity room. The family robot, Hoov, is on the computer.*
Hoov	Look! I've found some great short cuts on that racing game I downloaded yesterday! I'll show you how to get to level 9 really fast.

Pete   Brilliant!

Jenny   We're the best computer gamies in school because of you.

Mum   (*calling, irritated*) Hoov? Where are you?

Pete   Uh-oh. Have you forgotten to do something again?

list of chores:
breakfast things
vacuum
groceries
clothes
sky buggy

Hoov   Madam's list was: clear breakfast things, hoover everywhere except Master's office, order groceries on computer and … oh dear, refresh the clothes.

41

Jenny	It's always the same problem. As soon as you get near the computer, you start playing games and forget everything else.
Hoov	I don't mean to. I can't seem to stop. I was only going to see if I could get to level 9 on the racing game …
Mum	(*shouting*) HOOV! Where ARE you?
Pete	(*to Hoov*) Quick! Switch the game off before Mum sees.
Narrator	*Mum storms in.*
Hoov	(*standing up and bowing*) What is your wish, Madam?

Mum   My wish was to have the clothes
             refreshed! Why aren't they? I haven't
             anything clean to wear tomorrow!

Narrator   *Dad comes in, smiling.*

Dad   Hi, everybody. What's all the fuss?

Mum   Hi, love. Hoov hasn't finished his jobs
             again! That's three times this week!

Dad   I hope you've serviced
             my sky buggy, Hoov.

Hoov   (*groaning*) Uuurgh …

Dad   HOOV! I need it in the morning. I'm
             playing golf up in the sky sports park.

Hoov   I'm sorry. Very sorry. I'll refresh and service at once.

Narrator   *Hoov hurries out.*

Jenny   He is sorry. Don't be mad with him.

Mum   Oh, his 'being-sorry' programme works all right. But there's something wrong with his 'move-to-next-job' programme. There always has been, but it's getting worse. Maybe we should get him overhauled.

Dad   Programme overhaul on all-purpose robots costs a fortune. It would be better to get a new one.

Pete   What would happen to Hoov?

Dad   We'd take him to
           recycling.

Jenny and Pete   (*yelling*) NO!

Jenny   He's our friend!

Mum   He's just a robot. You'd
           get to like another one.

Pete   Hoov's special!

Dad   Well, don't panic. We can't afford a
           new robot right now.

Jenny and Pete   (*cheering*) Yay!

Mum   But if he doesn't get his wires together
           soon, we're going to start saving!

45

Scene

two

Narrator *When Pete and Jenny get up next morning, they find Hoov on the computer again.*

Pete You've downloaded a new game. Great!

Hoov It's a maze. Twenty levels!

Jenny Cool! Now don't forget your jobs while we're out today. Clear up breakfast, refresh beds, tidy house, recycle rubbish and contents of toilet tank, and prepare supper.

Pete   What a list! In the past, you'd have
been called a slave.

Hoov   Jobs aren't a problem.
I'm made for them.

Jenny   Wear my old thermal hat
to keep your brain
processor warm. It will stop the job
list from getting overridden.

Narrator *Jenny pulls the hat onto Hoov's head.*

Hoov   I'm not sure my brains are in my head.

Jenny   Wear it! You've got to stop upsetting
Mum and Dad. You've laid out
breakfast, haven't you?

Hoov (*groaning*) Oh dear. Why did I keep playing the new game?

Pete Quick! Into the kitchen before Mum and Dad come down!

Narrator *Pete and Jenny run ahead. They dash around putting things onto the table. When Dad enters, they freeze, smiling innocently.*

Dad You two look full of energy.

Narrator *Dad sits down, back to the door, without noticing Hoov is not in the kitchen.*

Dad I'll have coffee as soon as I've finished my orange juice, Hoov.

Narrator   *Jenny slips a hand behind her to switch on the coffee maker.*

Dad   I'll just check the weather in the sky sports park.

Narrator   *Dad presses a button beside the table. A large screen lights up on the wall showing a picture of the sky sports park. Hoov comes into the room, walking backwards. Pete and Jenny look at each other in horror. They turn him around.*

Information Service Voice

Temperatures are falling. But good news for gamies playing sky sports today. The sky sports park has been raised. It's now above the low cloud.

Dad   Terrific.

Narrator *Dad switches off the screen. Mum*
enters briskly and sits down.

Mum   We're late. I didn't
hear the wake-up
alarm. Did you set it, Hoov?

Pete   (*quickly*) I'm sure I heard it!

Mum   (*puzzled*) Well, hurry up if
you want a lift to school.

Narrator *Pete and Jenny sit down,*
looking worried.

Dad   Coffee now please, Hoov.

Hoov   Sir, now coffee.

Narrator *Hoov puts the coffee pot on the table.*
              Dad pours a cup.

Mum   Toast me two slices
              of bread, Hoov.

Hoov   Bread toast.

Narrator *Hoov takes the bread off the table and*
              puts it in the freezer. Everyone
              watches in disbelief. Then Hoov picks
              up Dad's full cup of coffee and pours
              it back into the pot.

Mum   He's completely lost it!

Pete   No, no, he hasn't! He's having a joke.

Jenny   We told him to.

Narrator   *Jenny whips the bread out of the freezer and into the toaster. Pete pours the coffee back into Dad's cup.*

Pete   (*faking a laugh*) We wanted to start the day with a bit of a laugh.

Dad   (*sternly*) I'm not laughing.

Hoov   Sir, sorry very.

Dad   Is he talking backwards?

Pete   We told him to act like he had a short circuit.

Mum   (*annoyed*) I'm going to be on a short circuit in a minute!

Hoov   Madam, sorry very.

Jenny   Hoov's going to stop joking
             now. All the jobs will be
             done PERFECTLY today,
             won't they, Hoov? He's got a hat to
             keep his brains warm.

Narrator *Jenny pulls Hoov's hat down further.*

Mum   Look at the time!

Dad   Is it that late? I should be on the first
             cloud tee!

Mum   (*angrily*) We'll have to
             miss breakfast. What
             a pantomime!

Hoov   Sorry very very.

Scene

three

Narrator   *Mum, Jenny and Pete arrive home late the same afternoon.*

Pete   (*coming in the door*) It's freezing in here!

Jenny   And there's a foul stink!

Mum   (*irritated*) The air control system must be faulty. Why hasn't Hoov checked it?

Jenny   (*as they walk through into the kitchen*) He's probably been busy recycling and cleaning and making a nice supper and...

Narrator   *They stop dead in the kitchen doorway and stare with open mouths at slurpy heaps of rubbish covering the table and floor.*

Mum   What the...? I don't believe it!

Pete   (*quickly*) Maybe the recycling system packed up and spewed out all this stuff.

Jenny   (*quickly*) And it accidentally got mixed up with the food for supper.

Pete   (*quickly*) And Hoov hasn't
            had time to clean it up yet.

Mum   (*shouting*) WHERE IS
            THAT ROBOT?

Hoov   (*groaning and muttering
            to himself*) Dear, oh.

Narrator *They look through the
            doorway and see Hoov
            on the computer
            in the activity room.
            He is so caught up playing the new
            game that he doesn't realise they have
            arrived home.*

Mum   There he is!

Narrator   *The front door slams. Dad strides in.*

Dad   (*shouting*) Hoov! Come here! (*he sees the mess*) What's happened? Where's Hoov?

Mum   (*pointing through the doorway*) In there! He's trashed the place and now he's sitting playing a computer game!

Dad   He forgot to put my sky buggy on charge overnight. It conked out. Jammed the whole sky sports park! I got fined! AND I had to pay a taxicopter to get it home.

Hoov   (*groaning as he plays the game*) Dear, oh! Dear, oh! This do can't I.

Mum   He's gone absolutely bananas. He's got to go!

Dad   Too right! I've checked and there's a good robot trade-in deal at Robots-R-Us.

Mum   Great! We'll take him in tomorrow!

Jenny and Pete   NO! Please, no!

Dad   Sorry, kids. His time is up.

Mum   No point asking him to deal with this slop. Come on, everybody help get it into the recycling tube.

Jenny   Oh, yuck!

Hoov (*groaning loudly as he plays the game*)
Dear, dear, oh! Wrong going is this.

Pete Listen to him groaning. Poor Hoov.

Jenny He must be sick. He's messing up the
game. The icon is
moving backwards.

Narrator *Jenny and Pete look
at each other.*

Jenny and Pete BACKWARDS!

Pete He's been doing everything
backwards today! I bet that
game's got a virus, and he's caught it!

Dad (*stopping work*) Could be. Come on,
we'll plug him into the virus cleaner.

Scene

4

four

Narrator *The family gather in the activity room while the virus cleaner gets to work on Hoov. When it is finished, they watch him anxiously.*

Dad Walk over to the computer, Hoov.

Pete He's going forwards!

Hoov   What a relief! My programmes aren't
              being overridden.

Jenny   You caught a backwards virus from
              that maze game.

Hoov   My processor records that two viruses
              have been cleared. A backwards virus
              and a games addiction virus.

Mum   Does this mean you're going to
              remember to do your jobs now?

Pete   One way to find out. Start level 1 of
              the racing game, Hoov.

Narrator *Hoov calls it up on the computer.*

Hoov   There you are.

Jenny   Don't you want to play?

Hoov   Not now. It's time to lay out
the supper.

Pete   (*shouting*) Yippee! You're cured!

Jenny   You don't need to keep your brains
warm anymore!

Narrator *Jenny whips off Hoov's hat and tosses
it to Pete who tosses it to Dad who
tosses it to Mum. Mum pulls it back
onto Hoov's head.*

Mum   Keep it on, Hoov. Just in case.